The New Adventures of
MARY-KATE & ASHLEY ™

The Case Of The
Creepy Castle

Look for more great books in

series:

The Case Of The Great Elephant Escape
The Case Of The Summer Camp Caper
The Case Of The Surfing Secret
The Case Of The Green Ghost
The Case Of The Big Scare Mountain Mystery
The Case Of The Slam Dunk Mystery
The Case Of The Rock Star's Secret
The Case Of The Cheerleading Camp Mystery
The Case Of The Flying Phantom
The Case Of The Creepy Castle

and coming soon
The Case Of The Golden Slipper

The New Adventures of
MARY-KATE & ASHLEY ™

The Case Of The
Creepy Castle

by Judy Katschke

HarperEntertainment
An Imprint of HarperCollins Publishers

A PARACHUTE PRESS BOOK

PARACHUTE PRESS

Parachute Publishing, L.L.C.
156 Fifth Avenue
New York, NY 10010

 **DUALSTAR PUBLICATIONS**

Dualstar Publications
c/o Thorne and Company
A Professional Law Corporation
1801 Century Park East
Los Angeles, CA 90067

HarperEntertainment

An Imprint of HarperCollins*Publishers*
10 East 53rd Street, New York, NY 10022–5299

1

SOME HALLOWEEN SURPRISES

"**I** still think we could have come up with better Halloween costumes," my twin sister, Ashley, told me.

I examined my costume in the mirror of our attic office. Wide-brimmed hat—check. Trenchcoat—check.

"What's wrong with our costumes?" I asked. "We're going as the Trenchcoat Twins!"

"That's the problem!" Ashley said. She gave the belt around her coat a tug. "It's not

a costume. We *are* the Trenchcoat Twins!"

Okay. She's right about that. My sister Ashley and I run the Olsen and Olsen Detective Agency. We do it from the attic of our house. Today, our attic was covered with paper cats, witches, and jack-o'-lanterns.

"That's what makes it a good joke," I said. "Besides, these costumes are super-easy. Next year we'll plan ahead." We'd been so busy solving our last case that we hadn't thought about Halloween costumes. We had almost forgotten Halloween was even coming.

Ashley adjusted her hat over her strawberry blond hair. "I guess these will have to do. It just seems weird wearing our trenchcoats when we have no mystery to solve," she said.

The words hit me like a ton of jack-o'-lanterns. It was Halloween. The most mysterious day of the year and there was no mystery to be solved! Anywhere!

Ashley knelt down to pet our basset hound, Clue. Clue was wearing a ruffled clown collar just for Halloween.

"It's a good thing we *don't* have a case today, Mary-Kate," Ashley said. "After all, Great-grandma Olive is coming all the way from Arizona to go trick-or-treating with us. She'll be here any minute."

Great-grandma Olive! Her name alone is enough to make me smile. She isn't just the coolest great-grandma in the world—she's also Olive Olsen, world-famous detective. Everything Ashley and I know about detective work we learned from Great-grandma Olive!

The doorbell rang and Clue barked. I glanced at the clock on my desk: It was six thirty P.M.

"I'll bet that's her!" I said.

Clue's floppy ears bounced as she chased us down the stairs. Ashley and I ran

so fast, we skipped steps!

"Who is it?" I shouted at the front door.

"Trick or treat! Smell my feet! Give me something good to eat!" someone shouted back. It was a voice I knew well.

Ashley flung the door open. Our friend Tim Park stood under the porch light, dressed as a scarecrow. He wore a straw hat, overalls, and a burlap pouch over his shoulder. Bunches of straw stuck out of his sleeves and collar.

"You can't ask us for candy, Tim," Ashley said. "You're going trick or treating with *us*!"

"It was worth a try," Tim said. He reached into his pocket and pulled out some small bags filled with candy corn. "Luckily, I got an early start."

Tim is the tallest and skinniest kid in our fifth-grade class. He also loves candy more than anything. No wonder Halloween is his favorite holiday.

"Where's Samantha?" I asked Tim.

"Here I am," cried a cute gray kitty. Samantha Samuels looked great as a cat. She had drawn a black nose and whiskers on her face. Her furry gray hood covered her curly red hair.

She hurried up the walk. "That cat suit is amazing," I told her.

"Thanks," Samantha said. "Mom made it for me." She turned to show me her long gray tail. It was attached to her furry one-piece suit.

Our next-door neighbor, Patty O'Leary, walked into our yard next. She was dressed as a ballerina in a tutu, tights, and a glittery crown.

"Princess Patty?" Samantha groaned. "You didn't tell me *she* was coming!"

I was surprised to see Patty, too. Ashley and I had asked Patty to come along—just to be polite. But Patty had told us she was going to Brianna Martinez's party. (Ashley

and I had really known that all along!)

"I know! I know what you're thinking," Patty said as she walked over. "You thought I wasn't coming. But Brianna and her brother have colds."

"Was the party canceled?" Samantha asked.

"No," Patty said. "But I'd rather go trick-or-treating than bob for apples with a bunch of runny noses!"

Oh, great, I thought.

Patty began to twirl around. "Don't you just love my prima ballerina costume?" she asked. "My father ordered it from a special dance store in New York City!"

Ashley and I rolled our eyes. We don't call Patty "Princess" for nothing! She gets everything she wants.

"It's really nice, Patty," I said. Anything to get her to stop twirling—she was making me dizzy!

Patty stopped. She stared at Ashley and

me. "And you two are...the Trenchcoat Twins?" She wrinkled her nose. "I don't get it. You *are* the Trenchcoat Twins!"

I felt Ashley glaring at me. Luckily, Great-grandma Olive's rented minivan pulled up just in time.

"She's here!" I cried, waving.

"Hi, Great-grandma Olive!" Ashley called out.

Great-grandma Olive parked the car in the driveway, opened the door, and stepped out. "Happy Halloween, kids!" she sang out.

Great-grandma Olive's long gray braid was tied with an orange-and-black ribbon. She was wearing jeans and a white sweater with black cats on it. But best of all were her earrings—dangly jack-o'-lanterns. Perfect for Halloween!

"I just flew in from Arizona and boy, are my arms tired!" Great-grandma Olive joked. She gave us big hugs.

"We missed you, Great-grandma," I said.

Ashley pointed to our friends. "These are our friends, Tim, Samantha, and Patty."

"Trick-or-treat team, ready to march!" Tim said.

Great-grandma Olive looked confused.

"Trick or treat?" she asked. "I'm sorry, kids. But I'm afraid we're not going trick-or-treating this year."

Everyone froze.

"What?" I gasped.

"No trick-or-treating?" Ashley asked. "On Halloween?"

2

CREEPY CASTLE

"**B**ut Great-grandma!" Ashley protested. "We always go trick-or-treating on Halloween!"

"Not this year!" Great-grandma Olive's eyes twinkled. "This year you're spending Halloween at Creepy Castle!"

"Cool!" we all yelled at the same time.

Creepy Castle is a haunted house that just opened up in town. It isn't a real haunted house. It's just for fun. But all kinds of weird things are supposed to happen there!

"We've seen commercials for Creepy Castle on TV," I told Great-grandma Olive.

"It looks awesome!" Ashley added. "Is it as cool as it seems?"

"I don't know. I've never been there," Great-grandma Olive said. "I made all the arrangements by phone. We're going to be the special guests of the owners, Max and Violetta Shudderly. They promised us lots of ghouls and goblins."

"And lots of candy?" Tim asked hopefully.

"Is that candy corn you're holding, Tim?" Great-grandma Olive cried. "I simply adore candy corn!"

Tim handed Great-grandma a small bag. "Knock yourself out, Mrs. Olsen," he said politely.

"Thank you, young man," Great-grandma Olive said. She waved her hand. "Now let's get this show on the road."

We quickly piled into Great-grandma Olive's minivan. I leaned back and took my

mini tape recorder from my pocket. Great-grandma Olive gave it to Ashley and me when we decided to become detectives.

I pressed the Record button and spoke into it. "Testing…one, two, three."

Great-grandma Olive smiled at me in the rearview mirror. "I thought you girls didn't have a mystery to solve today."

"We don't." I sighed as I clicked off the recorder.

"Hey, Mary-Kate, Ashley," Samantha said. "If you really want to solve a mystery, how about finding Minerva?"

"Who's Minerva?" Great-grandma Olive asked.

"Minerva's our class guinea pig," Ashley explained. "She disappeared from her cage yesterday."

"Poor Minerva," Patty said. "One minute she's eating cabbage in her cage. The next minute she's gone."

"So what do you say?" Tim asked, leaning

over his seat. "Is this a case for the Trenchcoat Twins?"

Ashley and I shook our heads. "Someone left Minerva's cage door open and she ran out," Ashley said. "No mystery there, right, Great-grandma?"

Great-grandma Olive nodded. "Sounds like an open-and-shut case to me," she said.

"Yeah," Tim said. "Someone left the cage door *open*, when it should have been *shut*!"

Great-grandma Olive drove about another two miles. Finally, she turned a corner and slowed down. "There it is, kids," she called out. "Creepy Castle!"

I pressed my nose against the window. The stone castle was covered with fake cobwebs and real ivy. Scary-looking goblins stared down from the tower.

Great-grandma Olive parked the minivan and we all climbed out.

"Check it out!" Tim shouted. He pointed to a tombstone in the front yard. "It says,

'Victor Veggie. Rest in Peas!'"

An evil laugh filled the air. It was coming from the castle! "May I borrow your tape recorder, Mary-Kate?" Tim asked. "I want to get all these sounds on tape. The kids at school will never believe it!"

I handed Tim the tape recorder as we walked toward Creepy Castle. "This place is huge!" I said.

"Actually, there are only three floors," Great-grandma Olive said. "The tower is what makes it look so big." She pointed to the dark tower on top of the castle.

"Does anyone ever go up there?" Samantha asked.

Great-grandma Olive nodded. "There's a long, winding staircase on the third floor that leads to the tower."

We stepped up to the front door. The porch creaked under our feet. Great-grandma Olive pressed the doorbell. Instead of a bell, there was a piercing scream!

Patty jumped back. "I-I-I think I can still make Brianna's party," she said shakily.

The door groaned as it opened. Standing in the doorway was a tall, pale man dressed in a butler's uniform.

"Greetings," he said. "I'm Skeeves, the butler. Follow me. Mr. and Mrs. Shudderly are *dying*...to meet you."

"Thank you kindly," Great-grandma Olive said.

We followed the butler through the front hallway to a pair of stained glass doors. Skeeves threw them open.

A smiling couple faced us. The man wore a black coat and a tall black hat. The woman was in a shredded wedding dress. Her veil seemed to be made of cobwebs.

"Welcome to Creepy Castle!" the man said.

"Thank you," Great-grandma Olive said. "You must be Max and Violetta Shudderly."

"You actually *live* in this place?" I asked

the Shudderlys. I couldn't believe it.

"Home sweet home," Max said with a smile.

We all walked inside. The parlor was filled with bulky old chairs. Large black stuffed birds were perched on shelves. Against one wall was a shiny black organ.

Max snapped his fingers at the organ. "Play us the 'Mummy Mambo'!" he said.

I leaned over and whispered to Ashley, "Who is he talking to? There's no one there!"

All at once the keys on the organ began to move up and down. We gasped and giggled as music filled the parlor.

"This place *is* fun!" Samantha said.

Skeeves served us spider-shaped cookies on a big silver platter. Violetta offered us purple boo-berry punch.

A bat on a spring dropped down from the ceiling. It flapped right in front of Patty's face.

"Eeeek!" Patty shrieked.

Max shrugged. "You never know who'll *drop* by!"

"Now finish your cookies, kids," Great-grandma Olive said. "So you can begin your tour of the castle."

"Aren't you coming with us, Great-grandma?" I asked.

"No," Great-grandma Olive said. "I have an important mystery to work on. I'll pick you up in three hours."

A mystery? I couldn't believe it. Why hadn't Great-grandma Olive asked Ashley and me to help?

But before I could ask, Great-grandma Olive blew us kisses and left the parlor.

"So!" Violetta said. "Are you ready to have a *screaming* good time?"

"Sure!" I said. "Where do we start?"

"Our son, Bradley, will get you on your way," Max said.

"Bradley, dear!" Violetta called. "Come

say hello to our new friends." A dark-haired boy appeared in the doorway. He was dressed in jeans. His T-shirt had the words *Prince of Creepy Castle* written across it.

I frowned. I knew that kid. He was Bradley *Austin*, the new boy in our class. I supposed Shudderly wasn't the family's real name.

"Hi, Bradley," I said.

He waved his hand and smiled shyly.

"Wow! I can't believe you live here," Ashley said as we followed him into the hallway.

"It's not exactly something I tell everybody," he said, not sounding too happy about it.

"I would," I said. "This is cool."

"Hey!" Patty said, pointing a finger at Bradley. "You're the one who cleaned out Minerva's cage in class yesterday. And you left the cage door open, too!"

"It was an accident!" Bradley said. "I

didn't know you had to shut the door *and* latch it."

I felt sorry for Bradley. It was hard enough being the new kid—without getting into trouble!

"It's okay," I said. "Accidents happen."

"Thanks," Bradley said. He looked around at all of us. "Are all of you friends?"

"Most of us," Samantha muttered. She looked at Patty from the corner of her eye.

Bradley heaved a big sigh. "I used to have friends...in my old neighborhood. We'd have a Halloween party every year. Then we'd all go trick-or-treating together."

Now I *really* felt sorry for Bradley.

Bradley smiled at Ashley and me. "Hey, neat! Twins dressing up as the Trenchcoat Twins!"

"Surprise!" Tim said. "Mary-Kate and Ashley *are* the Trenchcoat Twins!"

Bradley looked surprised. "You mean you're the famous detectives?" he asked us.

He crossed his arms. "No way!"

"Yes," Ashley said. "But today is our day off."

"Why don't you come with us, Bradley?" I asked. "To explore the castle."

"Explore? I live here, remember?" Bradley pointed to a steel door. "Start with that room in there."

I read the sign on the door. "Mad Lab?"

"Good luck," Bradley said as he walked away.

-I gave Ashley and our friends a thumbs-up sign. "This is it, you guys. Let's go for it!"

Tim clicked on the tape recorder. Patty gripped my elbow. I opened the door, and we stepped into the Mad Lab.

"Awesome!" I gasped as we looked around.

The Mad Lab looked like a real laboratory—only weirder. There were rows of bubbling test tubes and shelves full of stuffed bats, rats, and fanged snakes. I saw

jars filled with fake eyeballs, animal skulls, and brains. "All this place needs is a mad scientist," Samantha said.

"Did someone just call me?" a voice asked.

A man with wild hair popped up from behind a table covered with test tubes. He was dressed in a white lab coat splattered with dark red stains.

Tim pointed to the red stains. "Is that... is that—?"

"I'm afraid it is." The mad scientist sighed. "Tomato soup. I am *such* a slob!"

He handed us each a white card. It read: *Frank N. Stein. Body Builder!*

"Frank N. Stein? No way!" Tim cried. He ran over to a long white table. It looked like an operating table. "Is this where the Frankenstein monster came to life?"

"Yes, indeed!" Dr. Stein said, looking at the table. "Care to take a little ride?"

"Cool!" Tim slipped the tape recorder

into his pouch and hopped onto the table. "Just call me Tim-enstein!"

The mad scientist strapped Tim to the table. Then he grabbed a long wooden lever. It creaked as he pulled it all the way toward the ground. "Rise! Rise!" he called out.

The table began rising slowly toward the ceiling. Soon all I could see was Tim's hand waving down at us!

"Good thing he's not scared of being high up," I said.

Then something even stranger happened. The lights in the Mad Lab began to flash on and off.

"He's alive!" Dr. Stein cried. He pulled the lever back up. "He's alive! He's alive!" Ashley and I clutched each other as the table fell quickly back to the ground.

Hey, what was going on? The table was empty!

Tim was gone!

3

MISSING!

"**O**h boy," I said under my breath. The only thing left on the table was Tim's scarecrow pouch.

This place was *so* cool!

"What happened to Tim?" Ashley wondered out loud.

"He disappeared—that's what!" Patty said. She turned to the mad scientist. "And it's all your fault!"

"Calm down, Patty," I said with a smile. "This is all part of the fun!"

"Yeah," Ashley said. "Right, Dr. Stein?"

Dr. Stein shook his head. "Wrong!" he exclaimed. He looked worried. "I didn't do this. Nothing like this has ever happened before at Creepy Castle!"

"Are you kidding us?" Ashley asked. "Isn't this part of what happens when you come to Creepy Castle?"

"Honestly, it's not. I'm as baffled by this as you are," he replied.

I stared at the mad scientist. If *he* didn't make Tim disappear—then who did? Max? Violetta? Skeeves?

I ran my hand across the table, looking for a secret door. There were none.

"Yuck!" Samantha cried. She squeezed her nose. "What's that gross smell?"

I sniffed. Samantha was right. The lab smelled worse than our brother Trent's socks after a basketball game. But that wasn't the only strange thing that suddenly happened. The test tubes in the lab all

started bubbling over at once!

"Oh, no!" Dr. Stein groaned. "I knew I shouldn't have added that extra pinch of batwing!"

"Let's get out of here—please!" Patty shouted. She grabbed Samantha's hand, and the two dashed for the back door.

"Come on, Ashley," I said. "We're out of here, too."

"Wait!" Ashley said. She snatched Tim's scarecrow pouch off the table. "Okay. Now we can go."

Our feet pounded as we ran out of the lab and down the dark hallway. Skidding around a corner, we stopped in front of a rusty suit of armor.

I stared at the bulky suit. The helmet had a pointed top and a metal face cover. There was a long, thin scratch on the suit's front. In one hand, it held a rusty axe.

"We *all* could have disappeared in that weird lab," Samantha said. She sounded almost as worried as I felt.

"I *can't* disappear!" Patty wailed. She stomped her foot. "This costume has to be returned in three days!"

"There's got to be a way to explain this," I said. "After all, this is Creepy Castle! Weird things happen here all the time."

Ashley put her finger to her lips. "Mary-Kate, what's that noise?" she asked.

I listened and heard it too—a soft humming sound, coming from Tim's pouch. Ashley reached in and pulled out my mini tape recorder.

"Great!" Ashley said excitedly. She pointed to the green light. "It was on Record while Tim rode up on the table."

Ashley pressed the Rewind button. After a few seconds, she pressed Play. A deep voice came from the tape recorder. "Good evening," it said. "What just happened is *not* part of the fun at Creepy Castle. Do keep that in mind as you go on with your

visit. Mwah-ha-ha-ha-haaaaa!"

No one said a word.

My heart pounded as I clicked off the tape. Maybe we *weren't* welcome at Creepy Castle.

"I guess this wasn't part of the fun," I said slowly.

"Erase the tape." Samantha demanded. "It's creepy."

"No!" Ashley said. "It's the only clue we have!"

I looked at my sister. "Did you say 'clue,' Ashley?" I asked. "As in...a case?"

Ashley nodded. "Tim disappears. Then we hear a creepy message on the tape recorder. If that isn't a case for the Trenchcoat Twins—I don't know *what* is!"

I sure agreed. I wanted to find Tim. And now it seemed we hadn't worn our trench-coats for nothing! "I'll bet the Shudderlys have something to do with this!" I said.

"We don't know that for sure, Mary-

Kate," Ashley reminded me. I smiled. When it comes to solving mysteries, Ashley needs solid evidence to back her up. I like to go by my gut. If it feels right to me, I think it must be true.

"We should try to find the Shudderlys," Ashley said. "They might know what's happened to Tim. Let's go to the parlor and play the tape for them."

Ashley looked around. "There's only one problem," she said. "I can't remember where the parlor is."

CREAK! CREEEEEEAK! CREEEEEEAK!

I whirled around. Where did that noise come from?

Suddenly I saw something weird—the suit of armor had moved its arm. It pointed down the hall with its long, sharp axe!

Samantha must have seen it, too—her face was so white that her freckles were almost gone!

"M-Mary-Kate? A-Ashley?" Samantha

stammered. "That thing wasn't pointing a few seconds ago. Was it?"

"I'm not sure," Ashley said, staring at the knight. "But let's take his advice."

We followed the pointing axe and found the parlor. When we walked inside, Max and Violetta were not there. But we were not alone....

"I *knew* you were coming," a gray-haired witch cackled. She was dressed in a black cape and hat and was stirring a giant cauldron over the fire in the fireplace. "I could feel it in my warts!"

I stared at the witch. Was she a good witch or a bad witch? And more importantly—what did she know about Tim?

"Hello," Ashley said. "We're looking for our friend Tim. He's dressed as a scarecrow. Have you seen him?"

"No," the witch said. "But he must be doing his job well, because I don't see any crows around either!"

The witch rocked back and forth as she cackled.

"That's not funny!" Patty snapped.

The witch stopped laughing. "If you look closely, a clue might appear in my brew," she said.

Ashley and I peered into the cauldron. Chubby letters floated in a reddish-brown broth.

I shrugged. "Looks like alphabet soup to me."

"That's the whole idea!" the witch cackled. "The letters will spell out the answer to your question!"

"You mean...like magic?" Samantha gasped.

"Now you're talking!" The witch held out the big wooden handle. "Anyone want to help me stir?"

No one answered.

"I'll do it," Patty finally said with a sniff. "I took a junior chef course at the French

School of Cooking, you know."

The witch rolled her big eyes. "Honey, we're cooking eye of toad—not pie a la mode!"

Patty folded her arms angrily. The witch smiled and pointed to Samantha. "You can help me," she said. "A cat is always a witch's best friend."

"M-me?" Samantha squeaked.

The witch hooked her finger. "Here, kitty, kitty!"

Samantha gulped. She grabbed the wooden spoon and moved it in big circles.

"Bubble, bubble, boil to the brim!" the witch began to chant. "Help us find our good friend—Tim!"

Patty looked nervous. She backed up against the door.

"This is nuts," I whispered to Ashley. "There's no such thing as a magic br—"

I never finished my sentence. A thick souplike fog filled the room. It was so thick

that I couldn't see a thing!

"Mary-Kate!" Ashley called through the mist.

"I'm here!" I shouted back.

"So am I!" Patty yelled.

I expected Samantha to answer next—but she didn't!

"Samantha, are you there?" I demanded.

No answer. The fog began to thin out. I could see Ashley and Patty through the mist. But as I looked around the parlor I saw that the witch was gone.

And so was Samantha!

4

A Secret Message

"**S**amantha?" Ashley called.

"Come out, come out, wherever you are!" I called nervously. This couldn't be happening. Not again!

Ashley and I darted around the room. We looked for any way that the witch and Samantha might have slipped out.

"The window has a gate on it," Ashley observed.

"And I was standing by the door," Patty said. "They couldn't have gone out that way!"

"*MEOOOOWWW!*"

I froze as a gray cat strolled out from behind the cauldron. A *real* gray cat!

"S-S-Samantha?" Patty gulped.

"No way!" Ashley said, shaking her head.

I stared as the cat purred and rubbed her head against my leg. Samantha's cat costume *was* the same color as this cat. But that didn't mean the cat was Samantha.... Did it?

"That mean witch turned Samantha into a real cat!" Patty wailed.

"Patty, Samantha did *not* turn into a cat!" Ashley said firmly. "Those things only happen in cartoons."

"But Samantha *did* vanish, just like Tim," I pointed out. "Our friends are disappearing, one by one."

Ashley leaned over the cauldron and sighed. "I wish this brew really *was* magic. Then maybe it would tell us where Tim and Samantha are."

"Hey, Ashley," I said. I grabbed the spoon and began stirring the letters. "Maybe the answer *is* in the brew."

Ashley laughed. "Don't tell me you believe these letters are magic, Mary-Kate!"

"Not magic," I said. "A *message*! Maybe someone put those letters there for us to unscramble!"

"Hey, why didn't I think of that?" Ashley said with a smile. She reached into her trenchcoat pocket for her writing pad. As I called out each letter she wrote them down: S-B-O-K-O.

"KOBOS?...BOKOS?" I asked.

"KOOBS?" Ashley pondered. "SKOOB?"

"This is crazy!" Patty said, rolling her eyes.

"BOOKS!" I cried. "The letters spell out BOOKS!" I scratched my head. "But what do books have to do with Samantha and Tim?"

Ashley and I stared at the pad.

"It doesn't make sense yet," Ashley said. She slipped the pad into her pocket.

The organ struck a chord. We turned toward it. It began playing again—by itself!

"Let's go!" I said. The gray cat purred as the three of us ran out of the parlor and into the hall.

"I *hate* this old house!" Patty cried. "I should have gone to that Halloween party. *Any* Halloween party. Bobbing for apples in swamp water would be better than this!"

I grabbed Patty's shoulders and gave her a shake. "Snap out of it!" I demanded. "Great-grandma Olive says that detectives have to be brave at all times."

"Hel-lo?" Patty said. "You don't see me wearing a trenchcoat—do you?"

"Shh!" Ashley warned. "Here comes Bradley!"

Bradley was walking up the hall. I saw that he was carrying a crate piled high with droopy raw cabbage.

"Bradley!" I called as he came closer. "Hi. We're glad you're here. We have to ask you something important!"

Bradley didn't stop. "Can't!" he said, passing us by. "I'm eating my lunch now. I'm on a cabbage diet. It… uh…builds muscle. And I have to eat at certain times."

"It will only take a…" I called. But Bradley kept going and disappeared around a corner. When we turned the corner after him, he was gone.

There were four doors on either side of the hall. "He must have gone through one of these doors," I answered. I pulled on the nearest doorknob, but the door was locked. I tried them all. All locked. "I guess he had a key," I said.

The candles on the wall flickered as we went on down the dark gloomy hall. A shadowy figure stood at the end of the hall. As we got closer I saw who it was….

"It's that suit of armor!" I gasped. "It

moved from where it was before!"

"How do you know it's the same armor?" Patty asked.

"Check out the front," I said, pointing at the armor. "It has that same long scratch."

"I don't believe it," Patty said. "How did it get here? Walk?"

"It *could* walk if there was a real person in the armor," Ashley pointed out.

"Or maybe someone put it on a cart and moved it," I suggested.

"This is too weird," Ashley said. "First the armor was in front of the Mad Lab. Now he's by the…"

Ashley read the sign on the door. Then she gasped. "The library! He's in front of the library!"

"So?" I asked.

Ashley smiled at me. "So, libraries have *books*!"

"So?" Patty asked.

But *I* got it! The letters in the brew

spelled out "books." Maybe they were telling us to look for Samantha and Tim—in the library!

"We're going in there!" I declared.

"*AH-WOOOOOOOOO!*"

Ashley jumped and grabbed my arm. It was the longest, loudest howl I had ever heard—worse than the time I accidentally stepped on Clue's tail!

"I think it came from the library!" Ashley said.

"Maybe Samantha and Tim are hurt!" I gasped.

Ashley and I pushed the door open. Patty bumped into my back as we stumbled inside.

"Tim?" Ashley called.

"Samantha?" I called, looking around.

There were bookcases against the walls and a few portraits in between. A big chair with a high back faced a cheery, crackling fire. It looked like a normal library.

But Tim and Samantha weren't there.

"Yuck!" Patty exclaimed. She pointed to her dainty ballet slipper. "I just stepped on some gray fur, and it's sticking to my slipper. It's the same kind of fur that Samantha had on her dumb costume."

Ashley and I stared at Patty's slipper. The gray fur could mean Samantha was near.

Looking down, we saw a trail of it leading to the high-backed chair by the fireplace.

I didn't see any feet under the chair. But Samantha might have drawn them up under her. Was she sitting in that chair? And if so, why didn't she turn around?

Very quietly Ashley and I crept toward the chair.

"Samantha?" I called quietly. "Is that you?"

The chair began to spin around. When I saw who was sitting in it, I gasped.

THE WEREWOLF'S DATE

It wasn't Samantha. Or Tim.

It was a big hairy werewolf!

"Welcome!" The werewolf sat cross-legged on the chair. He grinned at us over the top of a book he held open in front of him. "I was just reading my favorite book, *Goodnight Moon*!"

My mouth must have hung open like a trap door. So that's where the gray fur came from.

"A werewolf!" Patty shrieked. "I'm

definitely going to faint!"

I could see that Ashley was trying hard to act brave. She threw back her shoulders and forced a smile.

"That can't be a *real* werewolf, Patty," Ashley said. "It's some guy in a hairy costume. Right, Mary-Kate?"

"Yeah, sure," I agreed. But I had to admit—that was one serious costume. And one serious *howl*!

"How can I help you girls?" the werewolf asked. "Are you looking for a book? A bestseller perhaps?"

I stepped forward. *It's only a costume… it's only a costume…it's only a costume…*I reminded myself.

I took a deep breath. "We were looking for our friends, Tim Park and Samantha Samuels," I said. "Have you seen them anywhere?"

The werewolf shook his fuzzy head. "I'm afraid not," he said. "But if I do, I'll be sure

to give a nice, big howl."

"Thank you," Ashley said.

"Now let's get out of here," I said quietly.

"Look!" Patty cried out. She ran over to a portrait hanging on the wall. "She's beautiful! Like a princess!"

The woman in the portrait wore an old-fashioned dress with puffy sleeves. Her hair was coiled around her ears, and she was smiling shyly out of a rose-covered cottage window.

"That was Caroline Shudderly." The werewolf sighed. "She was my date for the 1825 Harvest Moon Ball."

Just then I heard another creaking noise. Ashley must have heard it, too, because she gave a little jump.

"It's coming from the hallway," I said softly.

Ashley and I left Patty and the werewolf gazing at the portrait. We opened the door a crack and peeked out.

"Mary-Kate!" Ashley whispered. "The suit of armor outside the door—it's gone!"

I stared at the empty space by the door. It was gone all right.

"*Now* where did it go?" I asked.

We stepped into the hallway. Ashley bent over and picked up something white and orange.

"I don't know," she said. She lifted a piece of candy corn from the carpet. "But look what's in its place."

"Candy corn," I said slowly. "Tim's pockets were stuffed with candy corn."

Ashley nodded. "Is it a clue…or a warning?"

"Ashley," I gasped. "Maybe the *knight* has something to do with this! Maybe he knows where Tim and Samantha are."

"Or he might be the one who took them," Ashley added. "Now I'm sure someone is inside that suit of armor. But who?"

"Skeeves the butler!" I replied. "Don't

you remember those old detective movies we used to watch with Great-grandma Olive? The butler always did it!"

"Not this time, Mary-Kate," Ashley said. "That suit of armor is way too short. It would never fit Skeeves."

"True," I agreed, putting the piece of candy corn in my pocket. "But I still have a bad feeling about that knight—whoever he is. He keeps popping up wherever we go!"

"*AHHHH-WOOOOOOO!!!*"

There it was again—that bone-chilling howl. And it was coming from the library.

"Patty!" we gasped at the same time.

Ashley and I raced back into the library. Then we froze. The werewolf wasn't there. And neither was Patty!

"Oh, no!" I moaned. "Not Patty, too!"

If I didn't have goosebumps before, I sure had them now. Ashley and I quickly searched the library. We looked under chairs, a desk, even behind bookcases.

There were no hidden windows or secret doors. And there was no sign of Patty anywhere!

"How could she have disappeared?" Ashley cried. "We were standing in front of the door the whole time!"

"Maybe the guy in the hairy suit had something to do with it," I said. "Just like the witch might have made Samantha disappear."

"*HAHAHAHAHAHAHAHAHAHA!*"

"Ashley!" I scolded. "How can you laugh at a time like this?"

"I *didn't* laugh, Mary-Kate," Ashley said.

"You didn't?" I gulped. "Then who did?"

Ashley's hand shook as she pointed over my shoulder. I turned and stared at the portrait of Caroline Shudderly.

Her face looked completely different. Her soft, sweet smile had turned into an evil smirk!

6

A KNIGHT TO REMEMBER

That did it—now I was *really* spooked. How could a painting change like that?

"I know Halloween is all about tricks," I said. "But this one tops them all!"

Ashley and I stood shoulder to shoulder in front of the portrait. "Do you think Caroline is trying to tell us something?" Ashley asked.

"Yeah!" I answered. "That we should have gone trick-or-treating!"

I tilted my head as I studied the portrait.

Something else had changed. But what?

Then I saw it!

Before, Caroline Shudderly had been looking out of a cottage window. Now the cottage was gone, and she gazed out from a tower. A creepy gray tower that belonged on top of a castle!

I pointed it out to Ashley. "It's got to be a clue," I said. "Maybe someone is telling us that Tim and Samantha are up in the tower."

"But what if it's a trap?" Ashley asked.

"There's only one way to find out," I told my sister. "We have to find a way up to the tower of this castle."

We left the library and went out to the hall to look for stairs that might lead to a tower. We saw more creepy paintings and a big stuffed grizzly bear, but no stairs.

Ashley put her finger to her lips. "Shh! Quiet! I think I just heard something," she said in a low voice.

We held our breaths and listened.

CREAK! CREAK! CREEEEAAK!

"The knight!" I gasped. "Let's hide!"

We ducked behind the grizzly bear.

CREEEEEAK! CREEEEEAK!

The sound was getting louder and louder.

Ashley and I peeked out from under the bear's arm. I could see the suit of armor marching straight toward us!

The knight stopped next to the grizzly bear. His helmet squeaked as he moved his head from side to side.

My heart banged in my chest. *Uh-oh*, I thought. *He knows we're here.*

But the knight went on marching down the hall.

"There *is* someone in there!" I told my sister. "And I bet he knows something about the disappearances." It was another one of my gut feelings.

The knight turned the corner. "Let's follow him," Ashley said.

"I don't know if we should," I said. "That axe looks pretty scary."

"I bet it's fake," Ashley insisted, stepping into the hall. "Let's go."

We rushed down the hall. But when we reached the corner where the knight had turned, we didn't see him anymore.

"Where did he go?" Ashley asked.

I didn't have a clue. The only thing I saw was a staircase at the end of the hall. It had a heavy iron banister and a deep red carpet covering the stairs.

"He couldn't have run up the stairs that fast," I said. "Not in that tin can of a suit—"

"Good evening," a voice said from behind us.

Ashley and I spun around. A tall, pale man stood there. He was dressed in a long black cape. His hair was slicked back, and his lips were blood red.

Was it a real vampire? Or just a guy in a vampire costume?

I decided to go with the less scary choice.

"H-hi," I forced myself to say. "You didn't happen to see a knight go by…did you?"

The vampire heaved a big sigh. "Sad to say, I've seen *many* nights go by," he said. He nodded politely as he walked on. "Good evening."

The vampire's cape fluttered as he headed for the staircase. I frowned. Why did his voice sound so familiar?

"Mary-Kate," Ashley said. "Tell me those fangs were fake."

"Good evening. Good *evening*," I repeated. "*Good* eeeeevening!"

Ashley rolled her eyes. "Mary-Kate, you don't have to be *that* polite."

"No, Ashley," I said. "I'm trying to figure out where I've heard that vampire's voice before."

Ashley mouthed the words "Good evening." Then her eyes popped wide open.

"I know!" she said. "It's the same voice that was on the tape. The creepy voice!"

"Yes!" I cried. I spun around. The vampire was already at the top of the stairs.

"Stop!" Ashley shouted.

The vampire glanced over his shoulder. Then he turned and began to run.

Ashley and I raced toward him. But just as we were about to climb, something weird happened. The stairs flattened out—just like a gigantic wooden slide!

"Whoa!" I said, jumping back. "No way am I going to climb that thing."

"Me neither!" Ashley shuddered.

We looked around. There *had* to be another way to get up to the tower.

There was! Halfway down the hall was an old-fashioned elevator—the kind with a gate instead of a door.

Ashley and I pulled the gate open and stepped inside.

"This thing is old, all right," I said.

"There are no Up or Down buttons."

"Let's try this!" Ashley said. She grabbed a long wooden lever attached to the floor. She grunted as she pulled it all the way back.

The creaky old elevator began to rise. "Way to go, Ashley!" I cheered.

"Going up!" a scratchy recorded voice said. "Second floor—casual shrouds and formal shackles. Third floor—bats, gnats, and assorted rats!"

But after a few more seconds—
SCREEEEEECH!

The elevator stopped!

"Wha...?" I began to say.

"Going dooooooooown!" the voice said.

Ashley and I clung to each other. The elevator was plunging to the bottom!

"Ahhhhhhhhhh!" we screamed.

Bump! Ashley and I jerked as the elevator stopped.

"W-w-where are we?" I whispered.

"Basement level!" the scratchy voice announced.

Ashley and I gripped the gate and peered out. "Hmmm," Ashley said. "First the stairs, now the elevator. Mary-Kate, do you know what this means?"

"It means someone is trying to keep us from going upstairs," I said. "We must be right about the tower!"

7

TWIN MINUS ONE

We pulled the elevator gate open and stepped out.

"Wow!" I gasped as I looked around. The big musty basement was filled with all kinds of creepy stuff—fake tombstones, mummy cases, even a giant stuffed gorilla. It was lit by one flickering lantern.

"This must be the storage room," Ashley said.

"Or the dungeon!" I said.

The elevator gate slammed shut behind

us. We tried to pull it open, but it was stuck.

"Great," I cried. "Now we're trapped!"

Ashley shook her head. "There have got to be stairs around here."

We searched the damp, chilly basement and came across a door. It had a dark green frame and a black doorknob.

"I'll bet this leads to a staircase!" I said.

I flung the door open.

And jumped back in horror.

A mummy—wrapped in bandages—stood in the closet!

"So sorry!" I told the mummy and slammed the door shut again.

Ashley and I looked all over the basement for another way out. No luck!

"Boy, do I wish Great-grandma Olive hadn't left," I said. "We could sure use her help now!"

"She isn't here," Ashley said. "And we're not going anywhere right now. So let's figure

out what we know so far." She sat down on a wooden crate.

I began to count on my fingers. "First: Tim vanished in the Mad Lab. Then we found the creepy recorded message saying that it wasn't part of the fun."

Ashley went on. "Then Samantha disappeared and we got the clue that said 'books.' That led us to the library where Patty vanished."

"And don't forget the weird suit of armor that keeps following us around," I reminded her. "And the piece of candy corn we found where the armor was standing."

Ashley jumped up and began to pace. "There's also the tower in Caroline Shudderly's portrait," she said. "Which makes us think that our friends are being kept in a tower. But who's doing this—and why?"

"I think it could be Max and Violetta," I said. "They haven't been around too much

since this whole mess started."

"But what's their motive?" Ashley asked.

I pulled out my mini tape recorder. "Let's listen to the tape again," I said. "Maybe there's something we missed."

I held my finger on the Rewind button and waited.

"Stop!" Ashley said. "You're rewinding it too far."

"Whoops!" I stopped rewinding and pressed Play.

Ashley and I bent our heads as we listened. I expected to hear the vampire's voice. Instead I heard Tim!

"Hey!" Tim was saying. "What are *you* doing here?"

"Shhhh!" a voice replied in a whisper. "Just follow me."

Ashley and I stared at each other.

"Did you hear that?" I switched off the tape. "Tim said, 'What are *you* doing here?' As if he knew the other person!"

"Tim sounded surprised to see that person too," Ashley added. "Which pretty much rules out Max and Violetta. They live here."

I slipped the tape recorder into my pocket. "What a time to be stuck down here!" I said.

The elevator gate rattled as I shook it again. But it didn't even budge!

"Maybe we need something to pry it open," Ashley said.

"Like what?" I asked.

Ashley glanced around. A tall wooden wardrobe was standing against the wall.

"A coat hanger!" Ashley ran to the wardrobe and flung the door wide open. "Cool—this thing is full of clothes!"

The wooden bar was high, so Ashley stepped inside the wardrobe. She stood on tiptoes trying to reach a hanger.

I turned back to the gate and gave it another tug. And another. And another.

"Ashley?" I called back. "How about that hanger?"

No answer.

I turned around. Ashley wasn't standing inside the wardrobe. She wasn't standing *anywhere*!

"Ashley?" I shouted. I ran to the wardrobe and stuck my hands between the clothes. "Ashley? Where are you?"

I yanked dresses, coats, and capes out of the wardrobe until it was empty.

Completely empty!

"Oh, no!" I groaned to myself. "Not Ashley, too!"

8

THE HIDDEN STAIRS

My heart pounded so hard I could almost hear it. I searched everywhere for my sister—behind tombstones, under tables, even inside a big wicker basket. There was lots of dust and cobwebs. But no Ashley!

"Ashley!" I moaned out loud. "Wherever you are—I'm sorry I made you wear your trenchcoat on Halloween. If I find you, we'll wear whatever costume you want next year."

"Deal!" a voice called out from somewhere behind me.

I gasped. That was Ashley! But I couldn't see her anywhere!

"Ashley, where are you?" I said.

"Look inside the wardrobe!" Ashley's voice answered.

I raced back to the wardrobe and frowned. It was still empty. Until a section of the back wall slid open!

"Surprise!" Ashley said with a little wave.

I blinked hard. Ashley was standing inside a secret doorway. She pointed over her shoulder at a set of rickety wooden stairs.

"A door *and* a staircase," she said. "Are we lucky or what?"

I smiled back. "I guess Mom is right. You never know what you'll find when you clean out the closet!"

"There's just one big problem, Mary-

Kate," Ashley said. "The stairs back here are totally dark."

"No problem," I said. I ran to the lantern and lifted it high. "Now, let's get to that tower!"

Quickly I joined my sister on the secret staircase. The lantern lit the way as we climbed up three flights of stairs to the top.

"This must be the third floor," Ashley said.

Ashley pushed a door open. We stepped out into a dark hallway.

Through the gloom I saw cobwebs hanging from the ceiling. The wallpaper was dark green. A silver candleholder stood on top of a small table. Two doors stood on opposite sides of the hallway, facing each other.

"I just remembered something!" Ashley said. "When we were talking to Great-grandma Olive about the castle she told us that there's a door leading from the third

floor up to the tower."

I pointed to the two doors. "So which one will it be?" I asked. "Door number one...or door number two?"

One door was made of wood and it had a heavy latch. The other door was smaller and painted bright red. It had a paper sign on it that read KEEP OUT! THIS MEANS YOU!

"That one!" Ashley said, pointing to the red door.

As we rushed toward the door, Ashley stepped on something that crunched.

"What is it?" Ashley gulped, not looking down. "Bones? Fangs?"

I bent down and picked up a few scraps. They had a strong, sweet scent. I had smelled this before.... In school, in our guinea pig's cage! "These are cedar chips!" I said. "Like the kind Minerva has in her cage. Or *had* in her cage, anyway."

"Mary-Kate!" Ashley gasped. "You don't think they're holding Tim, Samantha, and

Patty in a cage, do you?"

"I sure hope not!" I said. I grabbed the door handle and gave it a twist. The door began to swing inward. That's when I heard a faint groaning noise.

"What was that?" Ashley asked.

The noise seemed to come from the ceiling. I looked up and screamed. Ashley screamed, too.

A giant spiderweb was dropping down from the ceiling—straight toward us!

9

BEHIND THE DOORS

Ashley pushed me out of the way just in time. I shivered as I stared at the big sticky web on the ground. Spiderwebs mean spiders. And boy, do I hate spiders!

"Someone was trying to keep us from going through that door," Ashley said.

That did it—now I was *mad*. "Nothing stops the Trenchcoat Twins!" I said. "Not even a dumb spiderweb!"

I shoved the door wide open. I expected to find stairs. Or maybe something horrible.

Instead I found a normal-looking room. A kid's room!

There was a bed covered by a bedspread with planets and stars on it. A desk by the window was piled high with notebooks. Shelves were filled with model cars and books. "This must be Bradley's room," I said.

Ashley kicked the spiderweb aside. "I guess he really likes privacy," she said.

I took a whiff and wrinkled my nose. "And cabbage!" I remembered all the cabbage he had been carrying the last time we saw him. "I guess he eats a lot of it for that health diet he's on."

After shutting the door, I turned to Ashley. "That leaves us with door number two."

I walked across the hall to the wooden door. Grunting, I lifted the latch and pushed it open. "Stairs!" I cried.

Ashley grabbed a candle from the can-

dleholder. We began to climb the long, dark, winding staircase.

"This staircase really turns round and round, just the way Great-grandma Olive told us it did," Ashley said.

"It sure does," I agreed. But then I had a strange thought. "Hey, Ashley? How did Great-grandma Olive know about these stairs? She said she was never here before, remember?"

"Who knows?" Ashley shrugged. "Maybe the Shudderlys told her on the phone."

I guess that's possible, I thought. I kept climbing the twisty stairs. They finally ended in front of another door—the door to the tower!

I was about to push the door open when I heard a chilling scream from behind the door.

"Oh, no!" I exclaimed. "They're hurting our friends. We have to save them!"

I handed the lantern to Ashley. Then I

reached into my pockets for a weapon. But all I found was the single piece of candy corn.

I opened the door, and we peeked inside.

"Are you seeing what I'm seeing?" Ashley whispered.

I sure was! Tim, Samantha, and Patty were sitting in comfy chairs and watching a monster movie on a big-screen TV. They were munching on candy and chips! Max and Violetta were there. So were the werewolf, the vampire, the witch, and Skeeves. Even the suit of armor was standing by a small stained-glass window.

"Pass the onion-and-garlic chips," Tim was saying.

"Garlic?" the vampire complained. "You really know how to hurt a guy, don't you?"

Tim leaned over for the chips. Then his eyes met mine. "Hey!" he cried. "It's Mary-Kate and Ashley!"

Everyone turned toward the door as we

slowly stepped inside.

"We didn't think you'd get to the tower for at least another hour," Patty said.

"Amazing," Samantha said. "You're really fast!"

I couldn't believe it either. Our friends had been expecting us all the time!

"You mean you guys set us up?" Ashley demanded. She jammed her candle into a brass candlestick.

Tim shook his head. "Not us," he said.

"Then who?" Ashley asked.

I glanced down at the candy corn in my hand. Then I remembered something else—there was only one other person I knew who loved candy corn as much as Tim.

"I think I know who," I told Ashley.

I marched right over to the suit of armor. "Knock, knock!" I said, rapping on its steel chest. "Time to come clean, Great-grandma Olive!"

"Great-grandma Olive?" Ashley gasped.

The knight reached up and pulled off its helmet.

"Great-grandma Olive!" Ashley cried. "It *is* you!"

"Well done, girls," Great-grandma Olive said with a big grin. "How did you figure out it was me?"

"It wasn't easy," I held up the candy corn and grinned. "Luckily, you dropped a little hint. We should have remembered that Tim wasn't the only one eating candy corn tonight."

"Whoops! You caught me." Great-grandma Olive laughed.

"Was this whole thing your idea?" Ashley asked her.

"Oh, yes," Great-grandma Olive said. "I planned everything with Max and Violetta, so you could have a mystery to solve on Halloween!" As she spoke, the Shudderlys grinned at us.

I smiled. What a *great* great-grandma!

"This armor was my own little trick," Great-grandma Olive went on. "I wanted to keep track of your progress without you seeing me."

Ashley turned to Tim, Samantha, and Patty. "Were you part of this plan, too?" she asked.

"Are you kidding?" Samantha cried. "Who could keep a secret like this? We were just as surprised as you were!"

"But how did you all disappear like that?" I asked.

Tim went first. "There was a trapdoor just above the Frankenstein table," he explained. "So when the lights in the Mad Lab flashed on and off, your great-grandma pulled me through the door."

"And I recorded that creepy message on the tape," the vampire said. "But you already figured that out." He reached into his mouth and pulled out his fangs. "I can't talk with these things!" he grumbled.

Everyone laughed—especially Ashley and me!

"My turn!" Samantha said. "When the fog filled the parlor, Zelda helped me vanish through another trap door."

The witch smiled and took a bow.

Patty pointed to the werewolf. "And he helped me disappear through a spinning bookcase. Right, Wolfy?"

"Under the watchful eyes of Caroline Shudderly," the werewolf said. He reached up and pulled the fuzzy gray mask off his head. "Man! This thing *itches*!"

I giggled. Underneath the fuzzy mask, the werewolf was just a normal guy with red hair and freckles.

"Speaking of Caroline Shudderly," Ashley said, "how did her portrait change like that?"

Violetta chuckled. "Oh, Caroline's portrait changes all the time," she said. "With a small flick of a switch."

"Girls, if I weren't wearing this armor I'd give you each a big hug!" Great-grandma Olive said. "I'm so proud of you two! You used all of your clues to find your friends in the tower!"

"Even though you did your best to stop us," Ashley said. "We almost got stuck in that giant spiderweb."

"And we would have gotten here sooner," I said. "If it weren't for that trick staircase and the runaway elevator!"

"Spiderweb?" Great-grandma Olive asked. She looked surprised. "Trick staircase? Runaway elevator? I had nothing to do with that!"

"Neither did Violetta and I," Max said, frowning. "Those tricks are mechanically controlled."

"And we haven't been in the control room since this afternoon," Violetta said. "What is going on here?"

"Mr. and Mrs. Shudderly?" Ashley asked.

"Who else in this house knows how to operate the mechanical controls?"

Max shrugged. "Just Violetta and myself."

I felt a shiver run down my spine. "But if you and Mrs. Shudderly didn't do all those creepy things—who did?"

BRADLEY'S GUEST

Ashley and I looked at each other. Who had tried to prevent us from getting to the tower?

Violetta spoke up. "You're all forgetting someone," she said. "Our Bradley. We did give him a key to the control room for his tenth birthday. And we taught him everything we know."

"He's made that bat drop from the ceiling before," Max said. "I bet he could figure out how to work the spiderweb, too."

Ashley moved toward the door. "I think it's time to find Bradley," she said.

Ashley led the way as we trooped back down to the third floor. We stopped in front of Bradley's door and the sign that read KEEP OUT! THIS MEANS YOU!

Ashley rapped on the door. "Bradley, are you in there?" she shouted.

The door opened a crack, and Bradley peeked out. "Yes?"

"Can we come in?" Ashley asked.

Bradley shook his head. "Um...my room is really messy."

"We don't mind," Ashley said.

"You should see our attic!" I added.

Suddenly I heard a soft scratching sound. It was coming from Bradley's side of the door!

"What's that noise?" I asked Bradley.

The scratching got louder.

"Um...er...mice?" Bradley gulped.

"Now, Bradley, dear," Violetta said. "We

may have bats. But no mice."

Ashley folded her arms across her chest. "You may not have mice," she said. "But I'm pretty sure you have a *pig*!"

"A pig?" everyone repeated.

My sister pointed to the cedar chips on the carpet. "A *guinea* pig!" she declared. "Minerva!"

My eyes widened. I couldn't believe it. So that's what Bradley was hiding in his room—our class pet!

"W-w-what are you talking about?" Bradley stammered.

"You have our class pet in there," Ashley said. "That's why you didn't want us going near your room!"

"Aha!" I said. "So that explains the trick staircase, the runaway elevator, and the spiderweb!"

"And all that cabbage!" Patty said, pinching her nose.

"Well, Bradley?" Ashley asked. "Do you

have Minerva in there or not?" We hadn't seen Minerva when we were in his room. But he might have hidden her in a closet, or taken her out of the room with him.

Bradley's face was red as he swung the door wide open. Our class guinea pig sat in the middle of the room nibbling on a piece of cabbage.

"Minerva!" Tim, Samantha, and Patty cheered.

"Bradley," Max said sternly. "I think you have some explaining to do."

Bradley leaned against the door and sighed. "Okay, okay. I didn't want Mary-Kate and Ashley near my room because I was hiding Minerva. I was afraid they'd find her because they're big-time detectives. So I sneaked into the control room and tried to stop them."

"How did you know where we were?" I asked, a little confused.

"There are video cameras all over the

house," Bradley explained. "I was watching you on a bunch of monitors."

"Wow!" Tim cried. "Just like mission control!"

"But why did you do it, Bradley?" Samantha asked. "Why did you take Minerva?"

Bradley waved his arms in the air. "I was lonely," he admitted. "It's not easy being the new kid in school. Especially when you live in a house like this!"

Violetta looked hurt. "What's wrong with our house?" she asked. "It's odd, but... interesting."

"What you did was wrong, Bradley," Max said. "And fooling with the controls could have been dangerous."

"I know," Bradley muttered. He stared down at his sneakers. "Now I'll never make new friends."

Everyone was quiet. Ashley and I looked at each other. Then we smiled at Bradley.

"You've already made friends, Bradley," I said. "Five new friends."

Bradley looked up. "You mean you guys?" he asked.

Ashley nodded. "But you have to do something first. You have to return Minerva to our classroom."

"We promise not to tell the teacher what you did," I told Bradley.

Violetta smiled at the twins and their friends. "Now that you and Bradley are all friends," she said, "does this mean you'll visit Creepy Castle more often?"

"Are you kidding?" Tim said. "This house would be great for a party."

"A *Halloween* party!" I added.

"A Halloween party?" Bradley gasped. "Here?"

"To the parlor, everyone!" Violetta said. "Party time!"

Everyone talked happily as we hurried down the stairs.

I turned to Great-grandma Olive. Her eyes were twinkling. She smiled at Ashley and me. "And I thought you girls would solve just *one* mystery today," she said.

I put my arm around Ashley's shoulder and smiled.

"Great-grandma Olive," I said. "When it comes to the Trenchcoat Twins—two is *always* better than one!"

Hi from both of us,

Ashley and I were about to live a true-life fairy tale. We were invited to a royal ball in honor of Princess Glorianna! Imagine meeting a real princess and staying in a real castle!

- But this fairy tale didn't seem to be heading for a happy ending. Princess Glorianna was kidnapped! It was up to Olsen and Olsen to find her in time for the ball.

Want to find out more? Take a look at the next page for a sneak peek at *The New Adventures of Mary-Kate & Ashley: The Case of the Golden Slipper.*

See you next time!

Mary-Kate Olsen

Ashley Olsen

A sneak peek at our next mystery…

The Case Of The
Golden Slipper

Bang! Bang! Bang!

My eyes flew opcn. I checked the clock. It was almost six A.M.

"Mary-Kate! Ashley! Wake up!" a voice cried. Someone banged on the door three more times.

I rushed to the door and jerked it open. Princess Glorianna's cousin, Serena, stood outside. She opened her mouth to speak. But she started to cry instead.

Ashley came up behind me. "What happened? What's wrong?" she asked. She gently pulled Serena into our room.

"Glorianna's missing!" Serena cried. She twisted the cloth of her nightgown in both hands. "And her room—it looks like she had a fight in there. It's all messed up."

"Let's take a look at the room you and the princess slept in last night," I said. "Maybe we can find some clues."

We flew down the hall. Then we ran up a flight of polished wooden stairs. Serena skidded to a stop in front of a door that had been painted gold.

"This is it," Serena said.

Ashley and I followed her inside. My heart started beating double-time as I looked around the room. A chair lay on its side. The bedspread had been torn off the bed. A china lamp had been shattered into a hundred pieces.

I hurried over to pick up the chair. I started to put it back into place. That's when I spotted a folded piece of light pink paper.

I carefully picked it up by the edges and opened it. Letters had been cut out of a magazine. Then they'd been glued to the sheet of paper to make sentences. "Ashley, you have to see this!" I called.

She rushed over. I held the note in front of her.

"Oh, no," she cried. "Princess Glorianna has been kidnapped!"

Your Invitation to Fun!

OWN THEM ALL ON VIDEO!

ALSO INCLUDES MARY-KATE & ASHLEY'S FAVORITE MUSIC VIDEOS

SCHOOL DANCE PARTY

A MUSICAL PARTY SERIES

Two Rockin' Episodes, All NEW School Dance and Our Music Video.

Greatest Parties

Three Pure-Party Episodes

Hand-Picked by Mary-Kate & Ashley Fans

Three Pure-Party Episodes
Hand-Picked by Mary-Kate & Ashley Fans

The Amazing Adventures of MARY-KATE & ASHLEY

Three Amazing Episodes
Hand-Picked by Mary-Kate & Ashley Fans

outta-site!
marykateandashley.com
Register Now

DUALSTAR VIDEO

GAME GIRLS.

MARY-KATE & ASHLEY'S
Magical Mystery Mall

October 2000

PlayStation

Available Now

Get a clue!
GAME BOY COLOR

DUALSTAR
INTERACTIVE

outta-site!
marykateandashley.com

RP
RATING PENDING
CONTENT RATED BY
ESRB

CLUB
AKlaim

Check out
the Reading Room on
marykateandashley.com
for an exclusive
online chapter preview
of our upcoming book!